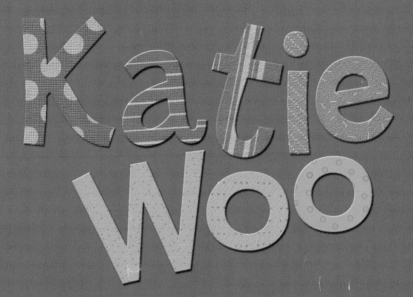

Katie Woo

The Tricky Tooth

by Fran Manushkin

illustrated by Tammie Lyon

PICTURE WINDOW BOOKS
a capstone imprint

Katie Woo is published by Picture Window Books,
151 Good Counsel Drive, P.O. Box 669
Mankato, Minnesota 56002
www.capstonepub.com

Library of Congress Cataloging-in-Publication Data
Manushkin, Fran.
The tricky tooth / by Fran Manushkin; illustrated by Tammie Lyon.
p. cm. — (Katie Woo)
ISBN 978-1-4048-6516-7 (library binding)
ISBN 978-1-4048-6611-9 (paperback)
[1. Teeth—Fiction. 2. Chinese Americans—Fiction.] I. Lyon, Tammie, ill. II. Title.
PZ7.M3195Tsi 2011
[E]—dc22   2010030648

Summary: Katie is the only one in her class who has not lost a tooth, but despite all of
her efforts, her wiggly tooth refuses to come out.

Art Director: Kay Fraser
Graphic Designer: Emily Harris
Production Specialist: Michelle Biedscheid

Photo Credits
Fran Manushkin, pg. 26
Tammie Lyon, pg. 26
Karon Dubke, pg. 31

Printed in the United States of America in Stevens Point, Wisconsin.
042011
006196R

Table of Contents

Chapter 1
A Loose Tooth

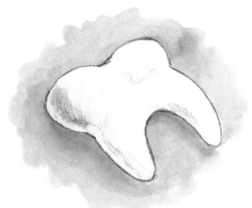

"Guess what?" Katie told JoJo. "I have a loose tooth!"

"So do I," said JoJo. "If we wiggle them, they might come out."

Katie wiggled her tooth

back and forth.

So did JoJo.

"No luck," said JoJo.

"No luck," sighed Katie.

"Let's eat a lot of popcorn," said Katie. "That will make our teeth come out."

The two of them chewed and chewed. JoJo's tooth fell out!

But Katie's stayed put.

At bedtime, Katie brushed
her tooth a lot, but it didn't
fall out.

"No tooth for the Tooth
Fairy," Katie sighed.

Chapter 2
Still No Luck

The next day, Miss Winkle

asked Katie's class, "Who has

lost a tooth?"

Everyone raised their

hands. Everyone but Katie.

After school, Katie played

soccer. She told Pedro, "I'll

hit the ball with my head.

That will make my tooth

come out!"

"I love the space between my teeth," Pedro said. "It helps me whistle really loud!"

Katie sighed. "I want a space, too."

When the ball came to

Katie, she bumped it hard.

She scored a goal!

But her tooth did not

budge.

The next day,

Katie lost a sock,

a button, and

her pencil.

But she did not lose her

tooth.

Katie's mom said, "Don't worry. Your tooth will come out when it's ready."

"I'm ready now!" said Katie.

Katie went to dance
class. She jumped and spun
around. She got very dizzy,
but her tooth didn't move.

At school, Miss Winkle made a tooth chart. "Put a check on it for each tooth you have lost," she said.

Katie had no checks.

At home, Katie told her dad, "I'd like to be a blue whale. They don't have any teeth to worry about."

"That's not a good idea," teased her dad. "Our bathtub isn't big enough."

Katie's mom told Katie,

"It's a mystery how teeth

come out."

"It sure is," Katie groaned.

"This tooth is tricky!"

Chapter 3

Way To Go!

The phone rang. It was

Pedro. He asked Katie, "When

can you come to see my new

puppy?"

"Right now!" said Katie.

"That will cheer me up!"

Pedro's puppy was
adorable! "His name is
Toto," said Pedro.

"Like in *The Wizard of
Oz*," said Katie. "Cool!"

"Can I hold Toto?" Katie asked.

"Sure!" Pedro nodded. "Just be gentle."

Toto was so warm and soft, Katie nuzzled him with her cheek.

"Arf!" The puppy barked
and nuzzled Katie back.

"Hey," said Katie, "I feel
something on my tongue."

"It's my tooth!" Katie yelled. "Way to go, Toto!"

"Way to go, Katie," said Pedro. "Now you have a space, too."

Katie couldn't stop smiling!

That night, Katie put the

tooth under her pillow.

"Don't fall out or anything,"

she said. "I want the Tooth

Fairy to find you."

And the Tooth Fairy did.

About the Author

Fran Manushkin is the author of many popular picture books, including *How Mama Brought the Spring; Baby, Come Out!; Latkes and Applesauce: A Hanukkah Story;* and *The Tushy Book.* There is a real Katie Woo — she's Fran's great-niece — but she never gets in half the trouble of the Katie Woo in the books. Fran writes on her beloved Mac computer in New York City, without the help of her two naughty cats, Gilda and Goldy.

About the Illustrator

Tammie Lyon began her love for drawing at a young age while sitting at the kitchen table with her dad. She continued her love of art and eventually attended the Columbus College of Art and Design, where she earned a bachelors degree in fine art. After a brief career as a professional ballet dancer, she decided to devote herself full time to illustration. Today she lives with her husband, Lee, in Cincinnati, Ohio. Her dogs, Gus and Dudley, keep her company as she works in her studio.

Glossary

adorable (uh-DOR-uh-buhl)—very sweet and lovable

budge (BUHJ)—move

gentle (JEN-tuhl)—not rough

goal (GOHL)—in soccer, the score made by sending the ball into the net

groaned (GROHND)—made a long, low sound to show unhappiness

sighed (SYED)—breathed out deeply to express sadness or relief

whistle (WISS-uhl)—to make a high, shrill sound by blowing air through your lips

Discussion Questions

1. How did Katie feel about not losing any teeth yet?

2. Katie tried lots of things to get her tooth to fall out. What were some of the things she tried? Can you think of any other ways people get teeth to fall out?

3. Have you ever lost a tooth? Did the Tooth Fairy visit?

Writing Prompts

1. Write down three facts about teeth. If you can't think of three, ask a grown-up to help you find some in a book or on the computer.

2. Did you know most sharks have five rows of teeth? Draw a picture of a shark, then write a sentence or two about your shark.

3. Katie and JoJo ate popcorn to try to make their loose teeth fall out. What other foods might make a loose tooth fall out? Write a list of five foods.

Having Fun with Katie Woo

In this book, Katie couldn't think about anything but losing a tooth. She thought about teeth at home, at school, at dance, and at soccer.

With teeth on her mind all the time, she would have loved this great "toothy" treat. Make your own mouthful of teeth. Before your start, wash your hands and ask a grown-up for help.

Toothy Treats

* Makes eight mouths

Ingredients:

- an apple
- peanut butter
- about 40 mini marshmallows

Other things you need:

- cutting board
- apple slicer
- paring knife
- butter knife

What you do:

1. Setting the apple down on the cutting board, use the apple slicer to cut the apple into eight equal slices.

2. Take each slice of apple, and cut it in half. You now have 16 pieces.

3. Spread one side of an apple slice with peanut butter. Place four to five marshmallows on top of the peanut butter.

4. Spread peanut butter on a second slice of apple. Place the peanut-butter side down on top of the marshmallows. Now you have a toothy grin!

Repeat until you have used all your apple slices. This is a tasty treat that is healthy, too!

THE FUN DOESN'T STOP HERE!

Discover more at www.capstonekids.com

- Videos & Contests
- Games & Puzzles
- Friends & Favorites
- Authors & Illustrators

Find cool websites and more books like this one at www.facthound.com. Just type in the Book ID: **9781404865167** and you're ready to go!